The Sticky Witch

by

Hilary McKay

Illustrated by Mike Phillips

First published in 2010 in Great Britain by
Barrington Stoke Ltd
18 Walker St, Edinburgh, EH3 7LP

www.barringtonstoke.co.uk

ISBN: 978-1-84299-770-3

Printed in Great Britain by Bell & Bain Ltd

AUTHOR ID

Name: Hilary McKay

Likes: Millions of things! Books, cats, honey, letters from readers (hint, hint), real music, apples, swimming in cold water, chocolate coated ginger biscuits, trees.

Dislikes: Putting things away, litter, loud TV, hot rooms, being told what to think.

3 words that best describe me:
Untidy, happy, hopeful!

A secret not many people know:
I am, and always have been, a VERY slow reader!

ILLUSTRATOR ID

Name: Mike Phillips

Likes: Cricket, books and my comfy chair.

Dislikes: Exercise, vegetables and sand in my shorts.

3 words that best describe me:
Short, round, fun.

A secret not many people know:
Don't tell anyone, but under my hat I've got no hair!

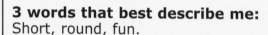

For Helena Cochrane, with love from Bella
and Hilary McKay

Visit Hilary's website at:
www.hilarymckay.co.uk

Contents

Chapter 1
The Raft

Tom, Ellie and Whiskers the Cat stood on the edge of the sea.

Tom had made up his mind to be brave.

Ellie had made up her mind not to fuss.

Whiskers had made up her mind to stay safe on dry land for ever and ever. She didn't like the look of the mad, tatty boat that was rocking to and fro out on the choppy green water.

The boat was a raft. Tom and Ellie's mum and dad had made it out of junk. They'd used the sort of junk that gets washed up on a beach. The deck was made of plastic bottles and worn-out tyres.

The ropes were old electric cables.

The sail was canvas from a long ago ship.

The cabin was a van that had fallen off a cliff.

Tom and Ellie's parents were going to sail around the world in the raft made of rubbish. "The raft will show everyone the rubbish that's been thrown into the sea. We're helping to save the planet," they said.

Tom and Ellie could see that saving the planet was a good thing to do.

"Also it'll be great fun," added their parents.

Tom and Ellie didn't think it would be great fun. Even so, if anyone had asked them if they'd rather sail round the world on a home-made raft, or stay behind with terrible Aunt Tab, they'd have chosen the raft. But no one did ask them.

"Children have to go to school," their parents told them kindly. "It's the law."

School's OK, thought Tom and Ellie. *We don't mind school. It's living with Aunt Tab that is not OK.*

They didn't feel like smiling but they had made up their minds to be brave and not fuss. So they looked out at their mum and dad on the sea and waved and tried to look happy.

"Good bye!" their parents shouted as they pulled up the anchor. "See you soon! Three years will go in a flash!"

The sail of the little raft filled with wind.

"Clean your teeth every morning!" shouted the parents. "Do your homework every night!"

The raft began to move, faster and faster.

"And write as often as you can!" shouted their parents.

And then they were gone.

Vanished.

In a moment.

Not a scrap of sail left to know where the raft had been.

Tom and Ellie stopped waving and smiling, and stared out to sea.

And as far as they could see there was nothing but sky and sunlight and wild green water.

"Sunk," said Ellie.

"No," said Tom.

"What then?" asked Ellie.

"Just gone, between one wave and another."

"I call that sunk," said Ellie, and she picked up Whiskers and hid her face in her soft, gold fur.

Neither of them said anything after that, but at last they grew tired of watching the empty sea, and turned back to the village. As they walked, Ellie thought of a hundred things. She thought about how useful it would be to have wings, or a life-boat, or normal parents. And Tom thought of one thing, which was that three years was a very long time indeed.

No cheerful thoughts came to either of them until they reached the village shop.

It had a rack of post cards outside.

"They said, 'write'!" remembered Tom.

"What?" asked Ellie.

"They said, 'write'," Tom said. "'As often as you can!' That *proves* they haven't sunk!"

"I don't see how," said Ellie.

"Think about it!" said Tom. "Would they have said, 'Write as often as you can!' if they were going to sink? No! They would have said, 'Don't bother to write!'"

"But ..." began Ellie, thinking at once of a hundred arguments.

"Help me choose a post card! Come on! Here's some cat ones. Do any of them look like Whiskers? What about this?"

"Too orange," said Ellie, looking.

"This then?" Tom picked out another post card.

"The cat in that picture doesn't have white paws," said Ellie.

"This?" asked Tom.

"Too thin. Perhaps this one?" Ellie picked up a post card of a golden tabby cat with stripes like a tiger and snow white paws.

"Wrong colour eyes," said Tom. "Not green enough. Never mind. It'll do. Come on, let's buy it."

They bought the card and wrote –

Dear Parents, if you have not sunk.

The news is that we hope very much that you haven't sunk.

With love from Ellie and Tom and Whiskers the cat.

and they addressed it to:

The Raft on the Way Round the World

If it has not sunk

Sea.

Then they put it into an empty lemonade bottle and ran back to the beach and threw it out to sea. Doing all this made Tom and Ellie feel much better.

But then they went home to Aunt Tab's, and that made them feel much worse.

Aunt Tab was not their real aunt. Tom and Ellie didn't have any real aunts. Aunt Tab was a person who had answered an advertisement from Tom and Ellie's parents.

This is what the advertisement had said:

Wanted

Extra special and very kind person to look after two wonderful children

And Whiskers the Cat

All expenses paid

In cash

A lot of people said they were happy to take care of Whiskers the Cat, and a few had said they'd look after *one* wonderful child.

One or two had agreed to have *two* wonderful children.

But only Aunt Tab had said she would have two wonderful children *and* Whiskers the Cat.

And so she was chosen.

Aunt Tab was going to look after Tom and Ellie while their parents sailed around the world. They had to move to her house and start at a new school, with new friends and new teachers.

Tom and Ellie and Whiskers had met Aunt Tab for the first time that morning. She had looked at them and said in a very grumpy way, "You don't look wonderful to me!"

So Ellie had replied, "Well, *you* don't look extra spe ...."

And Tom had pulled her out of the room just in time.

Aunt Tab's cottage was the last one in the village. She was waiting for them at the door as they came up the street.

"Well, well, so the good byes are over!" she said. "And the raft sank, I hear, almost at once! Dear, dear, never mind! As a matter of fact, I thought it might. Now, here are The Rules. A copy for each of you to carry about and two for your bedroom walls. I have also put one in the bathroom, and one in the kitchen.

The Rules were:

1. **No Fluff**

2. **No Crying**

3. **No asking Silly Questions**

4. **NO PLAYING IN MY PRIVATE POND.**

"That cat," said Aunt Tab, "is breaking Rule Number One already! It is *all* fluff! Must you keep her?"

"Of course we must!" cried Ellie. "Tom! Tom! Tell her we must keep her!"

"No crying!" snapped Aunt Tab. "Rule Number Two!"

Tom was very brave. "Of course we must keep Whiskers!" he said.

"Pity," said Aunt Tab. "I don't like fluff. And I detest whiskers."

"What's wrong with Whiskers?"

"No silly questions!" said Aunt Tab. "Rule Number Three! Stand still, little girl! There!"

Suddenly Aunt Tab had some huge scissors in her hands. *Snap!* they went. *Snap!*

And in seconds the messy orange plaits that had stuck out from Ellie's head for as long as she could remember were gone.

"PUT THEM BACK!" yelled Ellie.

"Don't be silly, dear," said Aunt Tab. "Now your brother!"

"What!"

Tom's ginger spikes flew into the air
Snap! Snap! Snap!

"There!"

Tom and Ellie grabbed their heads and stared. At each other. At Aunt Tab. At clever Whiskers, who had jumped up onto a high shelf.

"I'll sort the cat out later," said Aunt Tab. "Put a hat on if you get chilly! Now, dears, bed!"

"What, no supper?" asked Ellie.

"I thought you'd be much too upset to eat supper!" said Aunt Tab, in a very surprised voice. "Supper, after watching your parents sink before your eyes! How very, very hard-hearted!"

Still, she did make supper. Treacle sandwiches on sticky plates, and milk in sticky glasses. Tom and Ellie soon found that everything in Aunt Tab's house was sticky. The walls and the bathroom door knob. The mirror where they stared at their chopped-off hair. The sheets and pillows of their small chilly beds. It was as if everything had been rubbed or smoothed or touched or prodded by sticky fingers.

"Tom," whispered Ellie in bed that night, "do you think this is going to be all right?"

"Of course it's going to be all right," said Tom firmly. "It's just a bit sticky."

Chapter 2
The Treacle Pond

The first night at Aunt Tab's would have been awful without Whiskers. Tom and Ellie did not sleep well. First one, and then the other woke up and stared sadly into the dark.

Whiskers seemed to know how lonely they felt. She jumped onto their beds, warm and purring and not even a little bit sticky. Ever since she arrived at Aunt Tab's she had been washing herself. She was a clean cat, as well as kind.

"I don't see how Aunt Tab can't like her," said Ellie.

But Aunt Tab didn't like her. Not a bit.

"I've never seen such horrid fluff," she said when she poked her head round Ellie's bedroom door very early the next morning. "And I hope none of those awful whiskers are loose! If they are they will have to go, my dears! Snip, snap, and it will all be over! Now, children, a lovely breakfast is waiting downstairs in the kitchen ... Cornflakes. Eggs ... and treacle."

Ellie opened her mouth to protest, and then remembered about not fussing and closed it again.

"And then school ..." Aunt Tab went on. "And after school I thought a nice trip to the beach to look and see if anything's washed up from your parents' raft ... Did you groan, Tom dear?"

"No, I growled," said Tom.

"No growling please," said Aunt Tab and she smiled at him with her head on one side. "As I was saying, beach. Then homework. Then supper. Then bed."

"Let's run away," said Ellie, when she and Tom were alone in the kitchen, washing the sticky dishes after a very nasty breakfast. "How can I go to school with hair like this? And who will look after Whiskers while we are out? And I don't WANT to look for bits of raft on the beach! What if we find some?"

"We won't find any because they DIDN'T sink," said Tom. "I keep telling you that. And Whiskers will be OK. She's a clever cat. Nothing will happen to her while we're at school. Your hair looks quite nice, a bit like a bonfire. And we can't run away because we have nowhere to run to. I wish we had."

Ellie said nothing. She stacked the clean plates into a sticky cupboard and Tom picked up the spoons. They both felt gloomy.

Tom read the list of rules.

"What pond?" he asked.

"What?"

"What pond?" Tom asked again and pointed to Rule Number Four – **NO PLAYING IN MY PRIVATE POND!** "What pond? Where is it? And why is it private? That's what I want to know."

"Perhaps we'll find out at our new school," said Ellie. "That is, if anyone talks to us."

"Of course they will!"

"We'll be New," said Ellie. "Perhaps they won't."

Ellie need not have worried. Everyone had heard about the raft. Everyone knew where they were living. And they didn't have to worry about Whiskers. She came to school with them and everyone thought she was beautiful.

Loads of people talked to them.

"*You* may think her name is Aunt Tab," they said, "but *we* call her *The Sticky Witch*! Only don't tell her that. It's a secret. The pond is her treacle pond. Have you seen it yet?"

"No!" said Tom and Ellie.

"Well, you will," someone said. "She's always cleaning it out. She can't bear fluff in it. It blocks up the pump."

"What pump?" asked Tom.

"The treacle fountain pump," another boy said. "The fountain's on a little island right in the middle of the pond and the treacle bubbles out. It's very beautiful, if you like treacle."

"But what does Aunt Tab do with a treacle pond?" asked Ellie.

"Oh, the normal things," said the boy.

"*What* normal things?" Ellie and Tom both asked at once.

"Toads, mostly," the boy told them.

"Show us your treacle pond!" begged Ellie when she rushed home that night.

"I thought you were going to go down to the beach, dear," said Aunt Tab. "And see what is left of your parents' raft."

"There's nothing left," said Ellie.

"Fancy that, sunk without trace!" smiled Aunt Tab. "And how do you know about my treacle pond?"

"They told us at school! And they said your real name was ..."

"Yes?" asked Aunt Tab.

"They said your real name was a secret," said Tom, coming to the rescue just in time.

"So it is," said Aunt Tab, smiling a terrible sticky, witchy smile. "If I show you my pond will you promise not to paddle?"

"Oh, yes!" both Tom and Ellie said.

"And promise never to stir, lick, drink or dabble?"

"Yes, yes!" they said.

"And never let that cat go diving?" said Aunt Tab, glaring at Whiskers.

"Never, never," promised Ellie. She picked up Whiskers and hugged her.

"Very well then," said Aunt Tab, and led the way.

The pond was as round as a ring, with a flat, smooth edge of white stone. It glowed with a golden, sticky light.

"Is it very deep?" asked Tom.

"Very deep," said Aunt Tab. "Oh, yes, very!"

"There's a plug at the bottom. In the middle. See!"

In the middle there was a small stone island, in the shape of a water lily. From the middle of the island oozed a very slow

fountain. At the very edge of the island, as far as he could get from the fountain without falling in the pond, sat a toad.

"How did he get there?" asked Ellie.

"I put him there," replied Aunt Tab. "Long, long ago."

The fountain ran with golden treacle. And the pond was filled, right to the white stone rim, with golden treacle. There were splashes of treacle round the edge.

It was beautiful.

It was awful.

"You may dip in one finger," said Aunt Tab, smiling. "And have one suck."

They said, "No thank you, Aunt Tab," and backed away, shuddering.

"It is my great treasure," said Aunt Tab.

Dear Parents, (Tom and Ellie wrote on a post card of a sunflower – they couldn't find a post card of a pond)

Did you know there are 365 days in a year?

You said that you'd be back in 3 years.

That is 1095 days.

And 1095 nights.

So far we have done 2 days

And 1 night.

Love from Tom and Ellie and Whiskers the cat.

They put it in another bottle, and threw it out to sea.

"It isn't fussing, is it?" asked Ellie, as she watched the message bob away on the waves. "Or not being brave?"

"No," said Tom. "It's maths."

Chapter 3
The Toad

Days at Aunt Tab's began to fall into a pattern. School. Beach. Home. Bed. In between everything was treacle. Treacle meals. Treacle smells. Treacle stickiness.

Tom and Ellie got used to school and beach and home and bed but they never got used to the stickiness.

"It slows everything down," grumbled Tom.

That was true. You could not hurry on sticky floors.

Putting on school uniform, with sticky zips and cuffs and buttons, took a long time every morning. Sticky stairs, sticky taps in the bathroom, sticky curtains and sticky slippers slowed everything down at the end of the day.

Sticky homework took hours. Every night they washed their hands and wiped the table before they began, but still their pencils stuck to their fingers and their books had to be peeled from the table. It was worst of all when Aunt Tab came to watch.

"May I see?" she would ask, and reach a sticky arm over their backs and lift their books. "Very, very nice," she would murmur, and turn over the pages with sticky fingers. "Very well done!" and she would pat their heads and leave sticky tangles in their hair.

Ellie tried to make herself not mind the stickiness.

"It doesn't hurt," she said one day on the beach. "It doesn't sting. It doesn't tickle. It doesn't itch. It shouldn't be awful."

"It is awful," said Tom. "It's the worst thing in the world."

Ellie said the worst thing in the world was the way their parents' raft had vanished between one green wave and another.

Tom would not agree.

"We go to the beach every day," he said, "and we never find any bits of raft. Any day now we will hear from them. Then you'll see I'm right and they're perfectly safe."

Safer than us, thought Tom and looked at Aunt Tab. She was also on the beach, pouncing and prancing by the edge of the waves.

This day, more than ever, Tom wished that he and Ellie could run away.

At school that lunch-time they had heard a new story about Aunt Tab. A boy called Peter had told them.

The story was about the treacle pond. Peter was a new friend and he told the story when Tom and Ellie and Whiskers were sitting in the playground together.

"It was a long time ago," Peter said. "Last year, before you came. I was just outside the Sticky Witch's garden, behind the hedge. You know, the hedge at the end?"

Tom and Ellie (and Whiskers) nodded.

"I suppose I was being nosy. I was trying to see the treacle pond."

"Did you see it, then?" asked Tom.

"Yes," said Peter. "Yes, easily. I'd never seen it before and I thought it was amazing. It was much bigger than I thought it would be ... I suppose you've seen it?"

"Oh, yes," said Ellie.

"Did you notice the bit in the middle, the island in the shape of a water lily?"

"Yes," said Ellie.

"Well, two toads were sitting there. Right at the edge. One yellow, and one green. And the yellow toad said to the green toad ..."

"*What?*" shouted Tom and Ellie. "Toads can't talk!"

Peter ignored them. "... The yellow toad said to the green toad," he went on, "'How did you get here? Did you swim?'

'Swim? In that?' asked the green toad, looking at the treacle. 'I was chucked, that's how I got here. Chucked, in the middle of the night.'

'Same as me then,' said the yellow toad. 'What does she want us here for, anyway?'

'Thinks we'll grant her wishes,' said the green toad.

'Why would she think that?' asked the yellow one.

'Some toads can,' said the green."

Tom and Ellie's mouths hung open in shock, but Whiskers didn't look surprised at all. Perhaps she'd always known that some toads can talk, and that a few can even grant wishes. She was a very clever cat.

"'Some toads do wishes,' said the green one. 'Some don't. She doesn't know which we are. She's waiting to find out.'

'I know which I am,' said the yellow one. 'But I'm not waiting here till that Sticky Witch finds out. I'm going to swim for it!' That's what he said," said Peter and stroked Whiskers.

"Go on! Go on!" begged Tom and Ellie.

"Then the green toad looked at the yellow toad very sadly," went on Peter, "and he said, 'Don't. You won't make it.'"

"'Worth a try,' said the yellow one, and he slid into the treacle and started to swim."

"I didn't know you could swim in treacle," said Ellie, who was a good swimmer.

"I'd have thought it would be easier to jump it," said Tom, who was a very good jumper. "Toads can jump, can't they?"

"I don't know if they can jump that far," said Peter. "Anyway, the yellow toad didn't try. He swam. And he'd just got going (very slowly) when *she* came along."

"Aunt Tab?" asked Ellie.

"Yes. Her. The Sticky Witch. She came down the garden path towards the pond, smiling and singing ..."

"Oh," groaned Ellie, and Tom said, "I hate it when she sings."

"I wanted to run away," said Peter. "I was scared, all of a sudden. I don't know why, I hadn't done anything, only look through the hedge. She hadn't done anything, either, only smile and sing a bit, but still, I wanted to run away. But that toad was still swimming, and the other one was doing something very odd. He was hopping very fast from one side of the island to the other."

"He was trying to look like two toads," guessed Tom, and Ellie and Peter nodded.

"The other one was having an awful time. It was so hard to swim in that treacle," Peter went on. "Only his nose showed – like a tiny dark arrow. I thought the Sticky Witch hadn't seen him. She just kept smiling and humming and I kept watching and, very slowly, hardly moving, the yellow toad made it right across the pond. Right to the other side. And then he began climbing very, very slowly up the rim ..."

"Thank goodness," whispered Ellie.

"... and the treacle poured off him, and ran back into the pond. And his sides went in and out as if he was panting and the green toad hopped faster and faster and the Sticky

Witch smiled and hummed and stepped to the edge of the pond ..."

"Oh, no!" wailed Ellie.

"And she said, 'Silly.'"

"Silly?"

"And she poked him back in to the pond with the toe of her shoe ...

And he sank.

And the green toad in the middle went very still. But she was still smiling and humming. And then I must have made a sound ..."

"What sort of a sound?" asked Ellie.

"A scream, or something," said Peter.

"I'm not surprised!" said Tom.

"Because she saw me. The Sticky Witch came over to the hedge and she bent and peered at me and she laughed, and she said, 'Silly!'"

"Then what?

"Then I ran," said Peter.

Whiskers chose the card they bought after school that day. It was a picture of a toad on a lily leaf. Whiskers would not let them write on it. She carried it home in her teeth.

Chapter 4
In the Middle of the Night

Whiskers marched in front with her post card. Tom and Ellie walked behind her and talked about Peter's terrible story.

"Perhaps," said Ellie, "perhaps she thought she was being kind. Putting that yellow toad back into the pond. Perhaps she didn't know he would sink."

"Are you mad?" asked Tom.

"No I'm not," said Ellie. "It just makes her a bit less scary to think of her like that."

"Aunt Tab," said Tom in a very bossy voice, "is sticky! *Not* scary!"

Ellie didn't reply.

"I hope you're not turning into a scaredy cat," said Tom.

"I hope you're not turning into a much too clever, bossy pig," said Ellie.

It was the first time they'd had a quarrel.

They walked home in silence, sulking. They ate treacle pancakes sulking, and went to bed, still angry. Whiskers didn't like bad tempers. She didn't come and sit on their beds and purr. At bedtime she propped her post card up at the top of the stairs and sat beside it and glared at them.

It was hours before either of them guessed what she wanted them to do.

When Ellie guessed she shivered.

When Tom guessed his heart thumped hard and fast.

In the middle of the night, Ellie woke up. She thought Tom was asleep. She got out of bed and tiptoed down to the treacle pond.

Tom woke up too. He thought Ellie was asleep. He got out of bed and tiptoed down to the treacle pond. He went a different way.

They arrived at the pond the same moment.

"What are you doing here?" asked Tom, when he saw Ellie.

"I'm rescuing the toad," said Ellie. "What are you doing here?"

"I'm rescuing the toad," said Tom. "Where do you think Whiskers is?"

"I saw her outside Aunt Tab's bedroom door," said Ellie.

"She's keeping guard," guessed Tom.

They both felt a bit better at the thought of Whiskers keeping guard.

"Still, we'd better be quick," said Ellie, and they both turned to look at the pond.

Moonlight lit the surface. Silver light shone on the dark gold. They could see the toad, a lumpy shape in the middle. He looked a long way away.

"A bridge would be good," said Tom. "I think I might be able to jump it. But if I do I expect you'll say I'm being a much too clever, bossy pig."

"A boat would be good," said Ellie, "but I think I might be able to swim it. And if I don't try I expect you'll say I'm a scaredy cat so ..."

"NO!" shouted Tom, but Ellie was already in the treacle.

It clung to her skin like ropes. Ellie felt like a spoon stuck in honey. She felt like a fly trapped in a cobweb. She swam more and more slowly.

The treacle came up to her neck.

Then up to her chin.

Then up to her nose.

Ellie was choking in the gluey treacle. She couldn't make a sound.

Tom was too far behind to help. The lily leaf island was too far in front to reach. Ellie was sinking.

"Hang on!" called Tom, and jumped.

What a jump! From the rim of the pond to the lily leaf island! Tom was still too far away but something had changed. Ellie wasn't sinking any more. She was spinning. Slowly, then faster, round and round the lily leaf island.

Tom had pulled out the plug and Ellie was gurgling towards the plug hole in a whirl-pool of treacle.

Just in time, Ellie caught the stone edge of the lily leaf island.

First with her finger tips.

Then with her hands.

And then, with Tom's help, she was out of the treacle and sitting on the lily leaf.

With Tom.

And the toad.

All three of them were covered in treacle. They were glued and sticky and heavy with treacle.

"I couldn't jump back," said Tom.

"I couldn't swim back," said Ellie.

All around them, pale silver and dark gold, the treacle spun away.

"I had to pull the plug out," said Tom. "It was the only way I could think of to stop you sinking."

"Thank you," said Ellie. "It was a great jump."

"It was a brave swim," said Tom.

The pond became a pit. A dark steep pit, with sticky sides. They didn't feel at all safe sitting on the lily leaf fountain with its thin lily leaf stalk.

The last of the treacle glugged down the plug hole and the treacle fountain stopped.

"We'll just have to wait," said Ellie.

Chapter 5
Whiskers

Something moved on the far side of the pond.

A rustle.

And the sound of scrabbling feet.

It was Whiskers, the cleverest cat in the world. And she was dragging a hose pipe. When she got to the rim of the pond she picked up the end of the hose pipe in her teeth.

An arch of silver shot in the air.

Water, the only thing in the world that could save them.

It poured over Tom and Ellie. It poured over the toad.

All the stickiness was washed away.

And then they put the plug back in the treacle pond.

"The pond will fill with water," they told the toad, "and we'll be able to swim across. It is just a matter of waiting. And then you'll be rescued."

"And then I'll grant you three wishes," said the toad.

Tom and Ellie were so surprised they nearly fell off the lily leaf. Peter had told them that the toad could speak, but somehow they hadn't expected to really hear it. After all, he looked a very normal sort of toad.

"Wishes?" asked Tom. "Can you really grant wishes for people?"

"I can," said the toad. "As long as I am rescued first."

"Then why didn't you wish the yellow toad safe?" asked Ellie. "Why didn't you wish yourself away from the treacle pond? Why ...?"

"I can grant wishes for *other people*," said the toad. "Not for myself! Good grief, there wouldn't be a genie left in a bottle anywhere if people could grant wishes for themselves!"

"How unfair!" said Ellie.

"Not at all," said the toad. "It's the first rule of magic. I'm very surprised indeed that you don't know. However, since I can grant wishes for other people, you get three. One each, and one for the cat. I do think you might say ..."

"Thank you!" said Tom and Ellie together. "Oh, thank you! Thank you! But ..."

"Don't say 'but'," said the toad. "Get thinking, before the pond fills up and I swim away!"

At once, Tom and Ellie remembered what they had always planned. If they were ever given a wish, they'd wish that all the other wishes they wanted would come true. That would be a good way to turn one wish into hundreds.

"Cheating," said the toad, when he heard this plan. "Think again."

Tom thought of wishing they were safely off the lily leaf.

"That's a waste of a wish," said Ellie, "because we will be safely off, as soon as the water is deep enough to swim."

Ellie thought of wishing that their parents' raft hadn't sunk and that it never would.

"It hasn't and it won't," said Tom. "So that's a waste of a wish too."

"Yesterday," said Ellie, "we'd have wished for no more treacle."

"There is no more treacle," said Tom. "There's only a few splashes left. It's a waste to wish away a few splashes of treacle. It's getting light. Had you noticed?"

"I noticed the moon had gone," said Ellie.

"Morning is coming. It always comes in a rush, when it starts," said Tom.

It did come in a rush. One bird sang, and then a tree-ful. The sky turned pink.

"Very pretty," said the toad. "Now hurry up with those wishes!"

"I wouldn't mind being very pretty," said Ellie, looking at the sky.

"You look OK as you are," said Tom, kindly. "I wouldn't mind being fantastic at something. Like flying or football."

"You're already fantastic at jumping," said Ellie. "One fantastic is enough. Any more would be showing off. When shall we start swimming? Is it deep enough yet?"

"Soon," said Tom.

"Very soon," said the toad. "So get on with those wishes!"

Tom and Ellie began to make a list of things worth wishing for.

They thought of money in heaps.

Time travel.

World peace.

Being able to talk to animals.

And their own castle with a real moat and draw-bridge.

All the time that they were talking, Whiskers had the hose pipe in her teeth and was filling the treacle pond.

"Whiskers, Whiskers!" called Ellie. "Did you know you had a wish?"

Whiskers looked back at Ellie.

"Do you think she understands?" asked Ellie.

"Of course," said Tom. "She's the cleverest cat in the world. When will the wishes come true?"

"When I'm rescued," said the toad, and as he spoke the water lapped over the rim of the lily leaf.

The toad gave a great sigh of relief, slipped into the pond, and began to swim.

He was across in a moment.

Then over the rim.

And vanished into the shadows.

Rescued.

Gone.

"Safe," said Ellie. "Lovely! But how I wish the yellow toad had been saved too."

"Ellie!" groaned Tom.

"What?" asked Ellie.

Just then two happy croaks came from the bushes. "Nothing," said Tom. "Tell you later. Our turn now."

"Yes," agreed Ellie. "Come on!"

She jumped into the water and started swimming.

It was a moment before Tom followed. He was not such a good swimmer as Ellie, and he had a feeling that the water in the treacle pond was as cold as ice.

He was right.

"Oh," he gasped, as he slid off the island. "I wish it was a bit warmer."

Instantly, it became a bit warmer.

"Tom!" wailed Ellie. "Your wish is gone!"

"Well, so is yours!" said Tom.

"Mine? How?"

"The yellow toad! Didn't you hear? That was your wish!" Tom said.

"Oh!" gasped Ellie. "Oh, yes, of course! But still, if he is safe ..."

"We'll just have to do without wishes," said Tom.

It was not a good time to do without wishes. What Ellie and Tom hadn't noticed, as they splashed and wished and gasped, was a dark shape hurrying down the garden path.

There was no one to help poor Whiskers!
A moment later, she was grabbed by the
Sticky Witch.

"How many times do I have to tell you?
NO FLUFF NEAR MY TREACLE POND!" she
screeched. She swooped Whiskers high in the
air with a large sticky hand.

For a second, all the birds stopped
singing.

In that second, the morning sun suddenly
shone clear and warm on the treacle pond.

And then the Sticky Witch saw that the
pond was not golden anymore. It was a
bright, lovely blue, the colour of the sky.

And she saw that the only things in the
pond were two dripping wet, un-magical
children.

Her toad was gone, and all his wishes with him.

Then the Sticky Witch gripped Whiskers in a terrible grip, and she screeched and she hurled Whiskers high into the air.

Whiskers yowled.

Ellie and Tom wailed.

And then everything changed, because Whiskers had a wish to make too.

As she shot through the sky, this is what Whiskers wished. "I wish that toad would do something to help."

And he did.

By the time Tom and Ellie were safe on the ground, the magic had worked.

That was what the toad did to help.

Aunt Tab, the Sticky Witch, was a cat.

And Whiskers was Aunt Tab.

After that there was nothing left to do except live happily ever after.

Which wasn't difficult once they had cleared up the last of the treacle.

Aunt Tab was not a friendly pet cat. She was a thin, spitting, bad-tempered animal. Nothing ever tamed her. Not cream, nor kindness. She settled down a bit when Ellie had the good idea of giving her a saucer full of treacle. It looked a bit like her pond.

After that, every day, she sat by her saucer and growled if anyone came near. Then a circus came to the village and stole Aunt Tab. Ellie, Tom and Whiskers didn't miss her one bit.

Aunt Tab became very famous as the World's Stickiest Cat.

The treacle pond became a wild-life pond, full of happy toads, green ones and yellow ones. They didn't grant wishes. This didn't matter, because Tom and Ellie had nothing left to wish for. The same day that the wishes came true the postman arrived with a post card which he'd found on the beach washed up in a bottle.

Not sunk yet, it said. Thanks for all the post cards! Much love from Mum and Dad on the raft!

So that was all right.

Whiskers was a perfect aunt. She was merry, fluffy, and interested in everything. She never gave Tom or Ellie food made with treacle. In fact, she never made any food at all. Tom and Ellie soon became very good at cooking.

The Sticky Witch as a cat had many Sticky Witchish things about her. She was always hunting toads, and she still loved treacle. In the same way, Whiskers as an aunt had many Whiskerish things about her.

Even as an aunt, Whiskers had lovely soft whiskers and a swishing striped tail. Sometimes she washed her ears with her paws. Often she purred when the sun shone.

Sometimes she hardly seemed like a person at all.

Much more like a tiger sized, golden tabby cat.

The next three years went in a flash. All the post cards that Tom and Ellie sent were happy.

Having a lovely time.

So don't hurry back!

With love from Tom and Ellie and Whiskers the cat.

Barrington Stoke would like to thank all its readers for commenting on the manuscript before publication and in particular:

Nahid Ahmed
Olivia Alderman
Uchema Dmo-Bamawo
Sarah Gibson
Cathy Harrison
Olivia Alice House
Chris Hutchings
Marsha Ilina
Alima Khanam
Hafiza Khatun
Oliver Kidd
Louis Koffman
Zak Livingstone

Oliver Mathias
Lauren Metcalf
Tanbit Ahmed Miah
Khadija Mohammed
Faheema Mortuza
Pietra Piccinini
Avishai Sherman
Harry Stevenson
Sofia Strickland
Tamanna Tanzim
Piers Traulsen
Sara Ward
Hannah Weller

Become a Consultant!

Would you like to be a consultant? Ask your parent, carer or teacher to contact us at the email address below – we'd love to hear from them! They can also find out more by visiting our website.

schools@barringtonstoke.co.uk
www.barringtonstoke.co.uk